Max and the Gladiator

by Damian Harvey and Nigel Baines

W
FRANKLIN WATTS

Chapter 1

As Mum drove down the hill towards school, Max could see his teacher, Miss Anthony. She was standing inside a big blue coach and she didn't look very happy.

"Sorry I'm late Miss," said Max, as he climbed out of the car. "I forgot my packed lunch."

"You'd forget your head if it was loose," said Miss Anthony, giving her own head a shake. "Come and find a seat and we can set off. We've got a busy day ahead."

Max clambered on to the coach and made

his way down the aisle towards the back.

He could see his friend, Rajesh, waving at him.

Everyone was chatting excitedly about the trip.

Even Rajesh seemed excited.

"This is going to be cool," he said.

Max didn't know what all the fuss was about.

"We're only going to Chester," he said.

"I go there nearly every week with Mum and

Dad to do the shopping."

"This will be different though," said Rajesh.

"We're going to dress up like Roman soldiers and march around the city."

Max wasn't convinced. "It still sounds a bit boring. But I am glad to be out on a trip," he replied.

It wasn't long before their coach pulled into a big car park. Miss Anthony stood up and clapped her hands to get everyone's attention. "I know you're all excited," she said. "But we need to be sensible and keep together. I don't want anyone getting lost."

Max, Rajesh and the rest of the class followed Miss Anthony as she led them through the busy streets. Up ahead, Max spotted a huge Roman soldier standing in the middle of road.

Chapter 2

"My name is Titus Augustus," bellowed

the Roman soldier. "I'm a soldier in

the mighty Twentieth Legion. Today you will

do as I command." The soldier led them to

a museum where they put on plastic helmets

and small-sized armour.

"This isn't even real armour," Max complained,

putting on a helmet. "And this shield is tiny."

"Stop complaining," said Rajesh. "It's fun."

Titus Augustus told them how Emperor Claudius and his army had invaded Britain.

"We defeated the Celtic tribes and marched north," he said. "Here, we built a huge fortress and named it Deva Victrix."

Max, Rajesh and the rest of the class followed as Titus marched them through the centre of the city. When they reached the old walls, the soldier stopped. He told them the two walls that ran through the city had once surrounded the whole of the Roman fortress.

Finally, Titus led everyone through the city gates to the site of the Roman amphitheatre. He explained that it had been the biggest in Roman Britain. It was hard for Max to imagine how impressive it would have been. Half of the amphitheatre was still buried beneath the ground and the rest was in ruins.

It was almost time for lunch and everyone was sitting on the grass. Max was tired and hungry but Titus still had things to tell them. "Crowds of people came here to watch brave gladiators fighting each other," he said. "If you listen carefully, you can almost feel the swords crashing together."

The only thing Max felt was hot and tired.

It was a sunny day and marching with a shield and helmet was hard work, even if they were tiny!

Chapter 3

After eating his packed lunch, Max lay back
on the grass. He felt as though he could fall asleep
at any moment. But, just then, something caught
his eye. Titus Augustus was standing in the middle
of the amphitheatre. He was beckoning to Max.

Max sighed. He wanted to rest on the grass,
but obviously the soldier wanted to share more
fascinating facts.

Getting to his feet, Max saw the centurion walking towards the wall at the back of the amphitheatre. A large mural had been painted there to show how it might have looked hundreds of years ago. There was a door painted on the wall and as Max watched, the soldier walked right through it.

Max shook his head in disbelief.
"That's impossible!" he gasped. He looked round. Rajesh and the rest of the class were still sitting on the grass, eating their lunch and chatting. None of them seemed to have noticed what had just happened.

On the other side, the sunlight was blinding. Max screwed up his eyes as he ran forward, straight into something big and heavy. There was a thud as Max fell backwards on to the ground.

He opened his eyes in time to see a huge horse rearing up on its hind legs. The rider, struggling with the reins, shouted angrily at him.
"You clumsy fool!" he bellowed. "Watch where you're going."

When he had got the horse under control, the rider drew his sword and pointed it straight at Max.
"Arrest this boy," said the rider. Max felt hands grabbing his arms and dragging him to his feet.

17

Chapter 4

Suddenly, Titus Augustus stepped in front
of Max and bowed his head.

"Emperor Hadrian," said Titus. "I ask you to
spare this boy. I think he will prove to be
a great soldier."

Max stared in horror at the rider. He couldn't
believe he'd almost knocked Emperor Hadrian
off his horse!

The Emperor glared down at him. "Then he can prove how good he is by fighting my gladiator," he said.

As the Emperor rode off, Titus took Max by the arm. "You're lucky that the emperor didn't kill you then and there," Titus told him. "Let's hope you're as lucky in the arena."

"But I can't fight gladiators," cried Max.

"You have no choice," said Titus. "Today you fight in the arena. Tomorrow we march against the barbarians in the north."

"But I've got school tomorrow," said Max.

Titus wasn't listening. He was already on his way back into the amphitheatre.

Max looked around him. Only now did he
realise just how much everything around him had
changed. The familiar city of Chester was gone.
In its place stood a vast Roman fortress.

The walls loomed above everything and he could see Roman soldiers keeping lookout from the top. Instead of cars, the road was busy with horses and carts carrying food and huge blocks of stone towards the city gates. And there were Roman soldiers everywhere.

Suddenly, Max realised someone was shouting his name. Quickly, he stepped back through the doors and found himself in a cool, dark passageway. At the far end, he could see daylight and as he got closer, the sound of shouting grew louder.

Stepping into the sunlight, Max half-expected to see Miss Anthony and his friends. Instead, he found himself standing before a huge roaring crowd.

"I think they like you," said Titus, handing him a trident, a net and a sword. "You'd better not let them down."

Chapter 5

Max barely had time to look around. He could see the amphitheatre was no longer in ruins. It towered around him and was crowded with people. But what really grabbed his attention were the battling gladiators in the middle. One of them was holding a trident in one hand and a big net in the other. He was much bigger than the rest and defeated the others one by one.

Soon, he turned to face Max and started swinging his net above his head.

"First use your trident" called Titus. "Then your sword." But Max didn't listen. Instead he ran as fast as he could. The gladiator ran after him, and the crowd cheered even louder. Running in the hot sun with his armour on, Max was soon out of breath. He looked round and saw that the gladiator was getting closer. He realised that running wasn't going to save him ... he would have to stand and fight. They were now face to face with each other.

As the gladiator raised his net, Max remembered what Titus had told him. He raised his hand and threw his trident, then watched helplessly as it stuck into the ground in front of him. The gladiator threw his head back and laughed, but as he did his net got caught on the trident. The net swung around and wrapped itself round the gladiator's legs, sending him crashing to the floor at Max's feet.

Max quickly pointed his sword at the gladiator
and another huge cheer went up from the crowd.
When Emperor Hadrian got to his feet, everyone
fell silent.

"Very good," the Emperor called. "We don't often
get to laugh when gladiators do battle."
Before the Emperor turned to go, he tossed
something into the air. A small silver coin landed
at Max's feet. He popped the coin into his pocket
and flopped on to the floor, closing his eyes for
a moment. He'd never felt so tired in his whole life.

Suddenly, Max heard his name being called.

He opened his eyes expecting to see Titus … but instead, it was his friend Rajesh.

Max rubbed his eyes. Everything was back the way it had been. The amphitheatre was in ruins and Miss Anthony was gathering everyone together.

"I must have fallen asleep," said Max.

"Me too," laughed Rajesh. "I had a weird dream about being a gladiator."

Max put his hands into his pockets and was about to tell Rajesh about his dream when he found something. He frowned and looked down.

In his hand lay a shiny silver coin with the face of Emperor Hadrian on it.

Things to think about

1. Why isn't Max very excited by the school trip? How does it compare with how his friend, Rajesh, feels?
2. How does the Roman setting differ to the modern day?
3. What is Max's reaction when he sees the gladiator?
4. What might have happened if Max hadn't defeated the gladiator? Think about alternative endings.
5. How do you think Max feels at the end of the story? Support your answer with some evidence from the text.

Write it yourself

One of the themes in this story is time travel. Now try to write your own story with a similar theme.

Plan your story before you begin to write it.

Start off with a story map:

• a beginning to introduce the characters and where and when your story is set (the setting);

• a problem which the main characters will need to fix in the story;

• an ending where the problems are resolved.

Get writing! Try to vary the length of sentences to create drama and pace. Use interesting phrases such as "stared in horror" or "shook his head in disbelief" to describe your story world and excite your reader.

Notes for parents and carers

Independent reading

The aim of independent reading is to read this book with ease. This series is designed to provide an opportunity for your child to read for pleasure and enjoyment. These notes are written for you to help your child make the most of this book.

About the book

Max and his class are on a school trip to Chester to learn about the Romans. After lunch Max notices the tour guide beckon to him, so he follows ... and suddenly finds himself transported into a real Roman ampitheatre! Max must find a way to defeat the gladiator to have any hope of returning home.

Before reading

Ask your child why they have selected this book. Look at the title and blurb together. What do they think it will be about? Do they think they will like it?

During reading

Encourage your child to read independently. If they get stuck on a longer word, remind them that they can find syllable chunks that can be sounded out from left to right. They can also read on in the sentence and think about what would make sense.

After reading

Support comprehension by talking about the story. What happened?
Then help your child think about the messages in the book that go beyond the story, using the questions on the page opposite. Give your child a chance to respond to the story, asking:
Did you enjoy the story and why? Who was your favourite character?
What was your favourite part? What did you expect to happen at the end?

Franklin Watts
First published in Great Britain in 2018
by The Watts Publishing Group

Copyright © The Watts Publishing Group 2018
All rights reserved.

Series Editors: Jackie Hamley and Melanie Palmer
Series Advisors: Dr Sue Bodman and Glen Franklin
Series Designer: Peter Scoulding

A CIP catalogue record for this book is
available from the British Library.

ISBN 978 1445 1 6342 0 (hbk)
ISBN 978 1445 1 6343 7 (pbk)
ISBN 978 1445 1 6431 3 (library ebook)

Printed in China

Franklin Watts
An imprint of
Hachette Children's Group
Part of The Watts Publishing Group
Carmelite House
50 Victoria Embankment
London EC4Y 0DZ

An Hachette UK Company
www.hachette.co.uk

www.franklinwatts.co.uk

FSC
www.fsc.org
MIX
Paper from
responsible sources
FSC® C104740